THE MOOSE ON MY ROOF

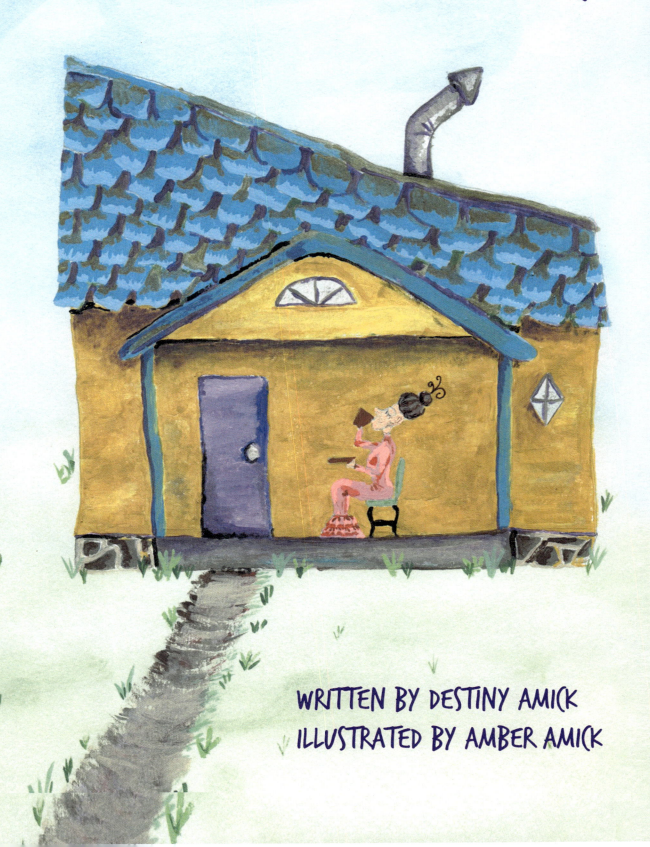

WRITTEN BY DESTINY AMICK
ILLUSTRATED BY AMBER AMICK

Copyright © 2016 by Destiny Amick. 742447

ISBN: Softcover 978-1-5245-0164-8
EBook 978-1-5245-0163-1

All rights reserved. No part of this book may be reproduced or transmitted in any form or by any means, electronic or mechanical, including photocopying, recording, or by any information storage and retrieval system, without permission in writing from the copyright owner.

This is a work of fiction. Names, characters, places and incidents either are the product of the author's imagination or are used fictitiously, and any resemblance to any actual persons, living or dead, events, or locales is entirely coincidental.

Print information available on the last page

Rev. date: 05/17/2016

To order additional copies of this book, contact:
Xlibris
1-888-795-4274
www.Xlibris.com
Orders@Xlibris.com

For all the children
who never really grew
up

The day before last while on my porch sipping my tea

I noticed something that until then had gone unnoticed by me.

Lounging atop my roof was a rather large moose.
At once I wondered if the screws in my head had come loose.
For how should a moose find himself perched on my roof?

And looking so aloof?

Perhaps he used a trampoline!
And perhaps that's why he's so fit and lean

Or maybe he used
a ladder
to escape the
neighbors chatter

Or found my roof by chance...

Hearing a clap of thunder
I decide to go inside to ponder.

Later in the afternoon a loud bang comes from overhead
that could wake the dead.

I slip my glasses on and go outside to see what's going on

I look up searching for the moose but
there is no moose on my roof.

Not an antler, not a hoof.

It wasn't a moose at all but a squirrel, small and furry

and obviously in a hurry.

Made in the USA
Columbia, SC
23 November 2021

49648527R00015